A YA Holiday Romance

I0594388

JENNI WARD

First published in 2021
by Miraworth Books
ABN 44 964 848 123

MIRAWORTH BOOKS
PO Box 3523, Mount Gambier, SA 5290, Australia

ISBN (e-book): 978-0-6488363-8-4
ISBN (paperback): 978-0-6453270-0-7

Cover illustration by Janenajla Arts
Cover typography by Miraworth Design
August Moon Romance logo © Jenni Ward, 2021

A catalogue record for this
book is available from the
National Library of Australia

Contents

Chapter 1

Mei

I liked how my sneakers didn't make a sound as I walked along the concrete pavement. Cars drove past, and I didn't doubt that they would have their air-conditioners on full blast. Not that I could blame them. Even as I glanced ahead, the path shimmered. For once, it would be a nice night at Elder Park for the Moon Lantern Festival.

Lao Lao loved the parade most of all and insisted I go with friends this year. She had broken her leg a week ago after, according to her, the step moved to test her and she failed. At first, I had been disappointed. Attending the festival with her had become our own mini tradition after she had moved from Beijing to live with us five years ago when Wai Gong passed away.

I loved having a grandparent around and she had taught me so much about Chinese culture. A lot of my friends in school just assumed because I looked a certain way, I must be an expert, but I had been born and raised in Adelaide and my life didn't seem all that different from anyone else's at school. Except maybe the food. Ma could cook the best dishes and most of them she had learnt as she grew up in China. My parents had moved to Australia to study at university; that's where they had met, fallen in love, and years later married and had me. They were still so much in love. I wanted to experience that mutual love one day.

Ahead, I saw Lucy as she waved her hand back and forth. Even after I waved back, she didn't stop. I guess she wanted to be sure I saw her. When I got closer, I saw her defending herself from blowflies. I sniffed the air; they were probably attracted to the perfume, which had an odd scent.

"Back off you evil winged creatures or I'll…"

Lucy didn't finish the word as her mouth slammed shut. She swiped at her mouth as a fly attempted to infiltrate it. The unusually warm weather so far in spring seemed to have triggered them to appear in numbers. At least the bus would provide some respite from them.

"Should have used the spray," I said as I stopped nearby. The flies stayed away from me.

"I didn't want it to mix with my new perfume, though," Lucy

said. Her pitch hit a new high as she squealed and swiped again.

I shook my head but couldn't but smile. The bus rumbled closer and Lucy stepped aboard as soon as the doors opened. We chose seats on one side and mainly sat in silence as the bus continued on its route into the heart of the city.

Our plan was to watch the parade and then check out the stalls, listen to some music, and watch the fireworks. Ma had allowed me to stay out until midnight since I was seventeen. Well, that was what she had said, but the truth was I knew she would like me home way before, or at least out of the city centre.

The bus stopped right outside the festival, so at least we couldn't get lost. Lucy got a map of where everything was as we entered through the gate. I glanced around and guessed that the festival had a similar layout to other years. Lao Lao had very specific of ideas of where to go when I came with her. *No matter, Lucy has a map; we don't need two.*

Elder Park had been transformed for the event. Paper lanterns were strung high above us and the trees had fairy-lights weaved through them. I cast my gaze towards the rotunda to see musicians chatting to its side; I loved listening to live music and one had a guqin. I had begged Ma for a guqin when I was about eight, determined to play the wooden instrument with seven strings. I had loved the idea of making the sliding tones. To me, it made the most beautiful soft music. Sadly, no one in the family could play one and when no tutor could be found, so they said no. Part of me still wanted to learn, though.

The music mixed with the chatter of people, as Lucy pulled me towards a stall with lanterns on poles. I gave her the money and told her to choose one for me; that was one less decision to make. My attention fell on another stall. That one hadn't been here the previous year, and I looked at the array of gold and silver jewellery.

"Hey, come on Mei, the sky is darkening and people are getting all the good spots," Lucy said.

She handed me a white lantern with a silhouette of a rabbit on the moon. I watched as Lucy held her own up to look at the dragon on hers. I glanced back at the other stall.

"These are so awesome." I felt her elbow attack my rib. "Girl, why are you looking at them? You know you can only get one if you actually open your mouth and talk to a guy first."

Sure, that's what the intention of the sets of jewellery might be, but that didn't make it an absolute.

I turned my gaze on Lucy. "Who says? Maybe best friends can do one too?"

The lantern bobbed up and down in her hand as she said, "You're right, friends over guys always, but do it later! Come on, we got a parade to watch."

It felt like I watched the parade with an overexcited seven-year-old. Every time people passed us by with giant lanterns in the shapes of moons and animals, she gushed about them and her phone worked overtime as she tried to snap half-decent photos to upload to social media later.

"That dragon got an upgrade from last year." Lucy sighed as we walked back into the park.

"Definitely got a bit of a makeover," I replied.

"Like you paid any attention at all. Don't go getting all coy with me. I saw you watching him."

"Who?" *Ma's right, I'm a terrible liar.*

"Hmm, let me see. It was a guy, tall, with shortish brown hair. You know, I believe you have science with him. Now, what's his name? Kevin, Kline, Kurtis..."

"Kane," I said.

"Ah, yes. Girl, why don't you just go and talk to him? Tell him you think he's hot? Ask him out?"

I shook my head. "There is no way I could ever do that. I mean, what if he's like: Who are you? I would never live that down."

"Being a teenager is all about making an idiot of yourself, Mei. Live dangerously just once," Lucy said. "Anyway, you guys watching each other when the other isn't looking is getting old."

"Well, we're getting old just standing here. So, whereabouts is Miki's stall?"

"Ah, let me see where I put the map."

Lucy came to a standstill and patted the sides of her jacket, then jean pockets. She arched her back a little to squeeze two fingers, with manicured nails painted neon green, into her jean pocket. They emerged holding a folded piece of paper. How she always managed to get the tight jeans on was a mystery to me. I also had many unanswered questions as to how her phone screen never cracked as she manoeuvred it in and out of the pocket.

"Okay," she said and unfolded the paper. Her index finger, well, the nail, ran across the page and she tapped on one spot. "That's hers there. Now, am I holding this in a logical way that we can just walk forward?"

My dark hair fell across my face as I tilted my head to get a better look. The map consisted of a bunch of numbers on a page showing the layout of the park for the event. Her nail pointed at number thirty-eight.

"I think if we turn the map to the side." I pointed to the

Torrens Lake. "That's over there, so the map should be like this. I think."

I rotated the map forty-five degrees and hoped I was right. The noise of the parade had replaced by the chatter of people as they lined up at the food stalls, which seemed to be everywhere. I glanced at the sky to see a mixture of red and orange that lingered on the horizon from the sunset. Once it was fully dark and close to the time in the advertisement, people would start securing their spots for the firework display.

"Okay, we'll go that way. If it's wrong, I'm totally blaming you," Lucy said.

"I wasn't the one who got lost last year on that orienteering hike at camp."

"Well, they should make the compass thingy easier to read."

We started to walk in the direction I had pointed. Once we got past the food stalls, the people thinned out and we could see the table ahead with Miki. She wore a red cheongsam with gold and silver flowers embroidered on it as she stood behind the table. At school last week, she told us it was only a cheap replica, as her mum wasn't convinced it would come back in one piece. Miki's mum was probably right considering Miki had a habit of sewing random pieces of fabric onto clothes whenever she felt inspired, or paint... and it wasn't always fabric paint either.

"Ah, my besties! About time you got here," Miki said.

"What do you have for us? You promised us something great," Lucy said.

"And I do. Oh ladies, I do have the best and most special of products for you tonight." Miki stretched her hands outs over the table. Hundreds of little bottles lined the surface of the table with sparkling liquid inside. There were several colours and my gaze fell on the pink ones as Miki picked one up and cleared her throat.

"Oh boy, we're about to hear the consequence of five years of theatre practise," Lucy said.

"Hey, the whole world is a stage and I'm sure my particular flair will help make some money. I want that pair of shoes I showed you last week. Now stop interrupting," Miki replied.

I admired Miki. The thought of being behind a stall and talking to complete strangers terrified me. Let alone putting on a show of drama that I suspected Miki was about to do. I envied her level of confidence around people.

"Here is the very elixir of life that the great goddess Chang'e stole away and drank to protect her loved one." Miki waved her hand over the bottle before she gave it a shake. The contents bubbled. "It was brought to us by divine work to put it in the hands of all those who wish to have good fortune in love."

Ying Yue, Miki's grandmother, who sat in a chair nearby, got to her feet and the blanket fell to the ground. She reached out for the walking stick that leaned against the side of the chair; her fingers tightened around the handle as she steadied herself.

"Hang on," Miki said. She placed the bottle back in its spot before she turned away from us.

"I am definitely getting a couple," Lucy said to me.

"Nai Nai, you are meant to rest," Miki said in Mandarin. "Come on, sit back down."

Ying Yue though, seemed to look at me. She had come from Beijing to Australia at the same time as Lao Lao and they had met on the plane. The corners of her lips curved up and more wrinkles appeared on her face. She shuffled forward until she reached the table. Behind her, Miki put her hands on her hips.

"Sorry, Ma asked her to come and keep an eye on me, but you know it's really the other way around. I mean guys, this is just lemonade, I swear," Miki said. "Just ignore her. Would you like to buy one?"

"Of course," Lucy replied. "Did you have to make so many colours? That makes the decision so much more difficult."

"I like the pink," I said.

I reached my hand out to choose from the pink bottles.

"No, no."

I raised my head and saw Miki's grandmother shake her head.

"Nai Nai, let her choose what she wants," Miki replied.

Miki's grandmother looked past me for a moment and her smile intensified as lines creased her forehead in determination.

"Ying Yue knows. You wait. Not that one," she said in Mandarin. Her wrinkled hand reached down under the table and I heard plastic bags rustle.

My plan had been to go to the parade on my own. Sometimes, when I was with my mates, it was difficult to do certain things without the fear of snide remarks or teasing. Of course, my plan had been torpedoed when Jace had turned up on my doorstep just as I had been ready to leave.

"The festival? Seriously, man? We could go to so many places tonight and that's where you want to go?" Jace complained as we walked towards the bus stop.

"You don't have to come; you invited yourself along."

When I turned to look at him, he had shoved his hands in his pockets. He shrugged.

"I guess it's better than doing nothing at all. So, what's the reason you want to go there, anyway?"

It was my turn to shrug. "Something different. You know, new experiences and all that. Plus, there'll be food there too."

15

"Ah, now there is something I can't argue with, man. I could polish off at least ten dim sims just for a start."

"You know that's more of an Aussie thing, right?"

"I don't care, they're delicious. Taste and stomach satisfaction is what matters most." Jace's shoulder connected with mine. "So, when did you become an expert on Chinese food?"

"Just something I read or heard on TV. I don't know, I can't remember." This was exactly the reason I wanted to go there alone.

"Ah, is this about the chick in science class? The one you've been trying to impress all year?" Jace turned and walked backwards in front of me with a stupid grin on his face. "It is! It's written all over your face!"

"Okay yes, maybe."

"Man, you are seriously going to a festival in the hopes that she will be there too? If you can't bring yourself to ask her out at school, then why go and do all this?"

"Because I like her, okay?" I sighed and stopped. "I just thought... I just thought I would..."

"So, you thought you'd make the effort, then?"

"Look, if you don't wanna come, no one is forcing you."

"And miss the chance to watch you awkwardly attempt to talk to her again? No way." Jace moved back around beside me, and we continued to walk to the bus stop. "What was her name again?"

"Mei," I replied.

"That's it. The last time you tried to talk to her was on that group project."

I cringed. That hadn't been my finest moment. I loved science, but I had been so focused on trying to impress her that I added the wrong chemical into the mixture. The end result being the entire school being evacuated and the fire trucks called. We'd spent an hour outside in the blistering heat waiting for the area to be cleared. Each time I walked past that table in science, I was reminded of that day.

We stopped at the bus stop, and I checked my watch. The bus was due any minute, so with any luck, it would be on time. I hoped the bus would be full of people who would chat away to drown out whatever Jace wanted to talk about. It wasn't my day, though. It pulled up half full, and those aboard weren't in a chatty mood.

"You know, Miki is cute. You think she'd go for me?"

"Go where?" I asked.

I sat down on a seat and felt it move as Jace plopped down beside me.

"Very funny. Come on, I have lots of qualities that chicks adore," Jace said. He struck a pose, and I debated whether to punch him.

"Remember, last year in drama class when you said Miki liked you?" I ventured, I shouldn't have, but if he could feel a little of my awkwardness, it would be worth it.

"Oh, you mean that thing where we all had to pretend to be another member of the class? Yeah, she chose me out of everyone."

"Why do you think that really was?"

"I'm freaking awesome. I mean dude, look at me, listen to me. If you don't want to be me, then you have terrible taste."

"Yeah, but that skit she did..."

"Was awesome!"

He had no hope. Seriously, Miki had clearly been sending him up in a hilarious fashion. Jace saw it as a compliment, but I had a feeling for Miki it was payback for all the obnoxious comments Jace had made. Like maybe she hoped he would hear himself and realise he sometimes came across as an idiot. I gave up.

The bus made its way through the busy streets towards the city. It would have been so much quicker if my parents would have let me take the car, but after my brother rear-ended a cop car last month, we both got put on restrictions. Instead of a comfortable ride, every time the bus went around a corner, I slid on the vinyl seat.

Thankfully for my ears, we were soon in the city. We got off the bus and began the walk towards Hyde Park. The sun was almost down, but the heat lingered fiercely for a spring day. At least this was a better way to spend the day than at school in a stuffy classroom or at home, as my sister attempted to sing with her headphones on, while thinking no one could hear her.

"So, you know for sure she'll be here, right?" Jace asked as we waited for the tram to move off before we crossed the road to the entrance gate.

"Pretty certain," I replied. Beside me, I saw Jace's eyebrows dance. "Yes, she is going to be here. I heard her and others making plans."

"My man has graduated to eavesdropping."

"I wasn't listening on purpose. They were at the next table and…" I sighed. I knew the more I said, the larger the hole I would dig myself into. "Just try to be normal, okay? Don't do anything, I don't know, weird."

Jace draped his arm around my shoulders and leaned in. "You do know who you are talking to? I mean, have you even known me to be sensible and not weird?"

"If I buy you food, will you at least shut up?"

I felt a hard slap on my back. Jace had a huge grin on his face that I accepted as a yes. We headed to a stall with Vietnamese food where Jace got five fried dim sims plus four vegetarian spring rolls. Good thing I worked weekends at the supermarket to pay for it all. The silence the food resulted in was worth the expense.

We weaved around others in the crowd as they bought food and headed towards some of the gift stalls. Ahead, I saw a table with little bottles on it. Miki stood next to a hunched woman that looked our way as she leaned on a walking stick. I couldn't see her eyes, but I shivered. The old woman smiled.

"Is it just me, or is that lady watching us?" I asked Jace.

"Wafing us?"

"Swallow first, then speak." We walked closer to the stall. "The lady over there."

"Ah, you mean that little old lady that just winked? Gee man, you got a real mature cougar about to chase you down."

"Jace..."

"Yeah?"

"Your mouth needs to be refilled."

"I'm happy to oblige."

He grabbed a dim sim from the white paper bag and shoved it whole in his mouth. It was like watching a toddler eat. I had first-hand experience after I did a work experience placement in a child care centre last term. It made me seriously consider if I ever wanted to work, or have children in my life... ever. The realisation that I had friends that resembled them grossed me out a bit.

I stopped walking and looked around. I must have been an idiot to think I would happen to come across Mei here. There were so many people mingling about the stalls that I began to wonder if I would see her.

"Come on, I reckon that lady wants a closer look at you," Jace said.

I rubbed my shoulder as he passed by me and walked ahead to the table the lady stood behind. A smile spread across her face as Jace approached. It felt wrong to cringe, but I couldn't stop the sigh.

I waited as a group of older people passed by. Jace had reached the table and was looking over whatever it was that they had on display in the bottles. I shoved my hands in my pockets and looked around. A couple of girls were already at the same table and I recognised Lucy from advanced maths.

As Miki put her hands on her hips, the older lady reached below the table. I knew who the girl beside Lucy was. Her long black hair flowed over her knit jumper and down her back.

"This is why you came," I said to myself.

I took a deep breath and walked towards the table.

"Hey Lucy, Miki, Mei," a voice called out.

I looked over my shoulder and felt my cheeks heat up. Kane and Jace were only a few steps away and headed for the same table. Jace got there first.

"I am thirsty as." Jace bent over the bottles.

"You should totally get glasses if you need to be that close," Miki said.

"Hey, I had to see if they were really that small. Come on, like I would have to buy ten just for a small drink."

"I won't object if you want to buy ten," Miki replied.

"I bet you wouldn't. What are these meant to be, anyway?" Jace picked up one bottle and gave it a shake.

Ying Yue's face looked up again as Kane stopped beside me. Her fingers were curled tight around something.

"Nai Nai, what are you doing?" Miki asked.

23

Ying Yue leaned closer to her granddaughter. "Elixir. Special."

"They want to pick their own," Miki replied.

"These." Ying Yue pointed to me and then Kane. Her fingers uncurled to reveal two bottles of sparkling liquid that looked very much like all the others on the table.

"Sorry guys, you can choose any you want. I don't know what's gotten in to her." Miki sighed.

"It's okay," Kane said.

He reached his hand towards Ying Yue with the coins in his palm, but she shook her head.

"Oh, let me give you..." I reached into my pocket to find my wallet.

"It's okay Mei; my treat," Ying Yue said in Mandarin.

I smiled and gave her a little nod as Kane took the two little bottles from Ying Yue's hand. I would have loved a pink one but didn't want to be rude, especially as Ying Yue seemed determined. I know if I refused such an offer, or went and bought another one, Lao Lao would be hurt.

"Xiè xiè," I said.

"Thanks," Kane said.

"May the moon guide your way on your journey to find what your heart holds." Ying Yue showed off her teeth as she grinned.

I had heard lots of phrases in Mandarin from Lao Lao, but that one I hadn't heard before.

The older lady smiled once more before her feet shuffled and she made her way back to the chair she had been in before. Ying Yue gripped the arms of the chair and lowered herself onto it. Miki already had a blanket in her hands as she draped it over her grandmother's lap as the old lady's eyes closed.

Lao Lao could fall asleep in an instant like that. I had often been talking to her as I wiped the dishes and would turn to find her asleep at the kitchen table. The little bottle felt cool in my hand as I turned it over and I wondered what Kane thought of the exchange.

"Hey, the fireworks are going to start soon," Lucy said.

I looked up from the bottle as Lucy grabbed my arm and tugged me towards the grassed area.

"Come on Mei, I'm not going to miss them and I want to get a good view that doesn't have a hundred people crowding around me." Lucy paused and smiled. She tilted her head to the side and her long blond ponytail swung back and forth. "You know Kane, you and Jace could join us too, if you wanted."

My cheeks burned. I felt Lucy's grip loosen on my arm as a couple of friends waved in the distance.

"Sure, I'm in. Jace, you finished eating for a bit?" Kane said behind me.

"Let me just grab a serve from that stall with the circle cake thingys."

"Mooncakes?" I said.

He waved his finger. "That's the one. Don't worry, I'll catch up in like a second. I promise you won't even miss me," Jace replied.

I glanced over my shoulder in time to see Jace weave back into the crowd and disappear. Kane came into view as he stepped around beside me.

"On the upside, we will have a moment's peace while he's gone," Kane said.

"Come on then, the others are waiting." Lucy ran ahead, which left me alone with Kane, and I doubted that was an accident.

"After you Mei," Kane said.

I tucked my hair behind my ear as I smiled. We followed together behind Lucy, who had already staked her territory for our viewing area. The others had all sat down, but they left enough space on the end for Kane and me to sit... together.

After I sat down, I checked my phone to see we only had a few minutes until the fireworks would begin. Every time Kane moved, I felt hyper-aware of the slightest touch. I kept my head lowered so my hair could form a curtain around my face. I wanted to glance over at him and smile, but every time I thought about doing it, my heart pounded in my chest and I chickened out.

Instead, I focused on the bottle in my hand. The liquid moved slowly inside as I rolled the glass back and forth on my palm.

"What do you think it is?" Kane asked.

I looked away from my little bottle to see he had his in his hand as well.

"Oh, Miki said the other day it was just going to be lemonade," I said.

Still, I had my doubts. I gave the bottle a little shake and watched the bubbles appear and rise to the top. I guess that and a bit of food colouring can go a long way. Still, I keep looking at it and wondered if Miki's grandmother had put something else into it. You know, the way she insisted we have these two instead of the others.

I smiled. "It may have something for flavour, but I don't think we need to worry. Maybe these are sweeter than the others? Miki knows I'm not fond of anything really bitter."

"Ah well, if it means we got the best of the lemonade, then we should enjoy it."

27

"Elixir, remember," I corrected him.

The bubbles continued to rise to the surface as I twisted the lid off the bottle. I sniffed. It smelt like lemonade. It sort of looked like lemonade. *It probably is just lemonade, right?*

"Well, it doesn't smell weird," Kane said beside me. "Definitely a lemonadey-smell with... I think I can detect a hint of ginger. My mum is always adding ginger to things, even though my dad hates it."

"Are we being overly cautious over a drink?" I asked.

"Probably. You're friends with Miki, right? I mean, it's not like you suspect she is some evil teenager with an equally underhanded grandmother serial killer who intends on poisoning us."

"You make a valid point."

Kane raised the lemonade up and peered at it as he swooshed it around. "Looks to me like a very fine concoction, miss. Shall we toast to the moon and enjoy?"

"I think we shall. To the tragic tale of Chang'e and Hou Yi. May love always guide them though they are separated."

"To love."

From between the strands of hair, I saw that Kane blushed at the word. I doubted he had intended to say it out loud. He tipped the contents of the bottle into his mouth in one go. Ma would not be happy if I did that. I put the bottle to my lips and felt the thick, slightly bubbly liquid enter my mouth. It wasn't unpleasant to swallow it, but it didn't taste like any lemonade I had drunk before.

My hand lowered as I heard the first of the fireworks whirl into the sky. Red tones filled the sky as one, two, then three exploded. *Why are they so loud?* I didn't recall fireworks ever being so loud, even on New Year's eve.

The bottle fell to the grass beside me. I tried to focus on the fireworks, but they blurred into the night sky. My hand rested on my forehead as I glanced away from the blurred sky. Nothing in front of me looked any clearer. Lucy's hair was a blob. I turned my head to look at Kane. He at least looked clear, but the background swirled behind him and made me feel sick.

"Mei?"

I knew Kane said it and yet it sounded like my head was under water. And then everything came into focus again, except it wasn't right.

...could not hang on to mad and ... me. The branches and twisting they slowly pulled apart ... ...much ... ... going back but nothing that ... ... it ... had it not been ...

My hand reached as it being the ... ... slowly that him flashed ... toward him to ... ... it ... went ... she ... Within a year or so I ... ... it blew out of its hole ... under the grey ...

The birth of the ... was very little ... ... the tree ... but one married him ... ... she might be helped many branches that spread ... ... it ... nothing ... through all the patient and even ... ... to ... ... another bird who was part of anything and ... Kachina would swirl it ... ...

"Me."

"I know Kathi." ... him and ... ... water. And then ... ... it.

Chapter 4
Kane

"Where is everybody?" I said.

The people who had been all around me on blankets were gone; so were the blankets. My head pounded, but at least normal sounds had replaced the muffled ones. When I turned to look beside me, I saw Mei. She turned around on the spot, probably as confused as I was. The people were gone, the chatter silenced, the smell of food lingered though.

I twisted around so I could look behind us. The grass spread out towards the stalls...

"That's interesting," I murmured.

I pushed myself to my feet. Everyone except Mei and me was gone, and yet some things remained. Mei moved beside me and I looked down. She had turned to look in the same direction as I had. I reached my hand down, and she took it as she stood beside me.

"They were just here and then…" Mei paused and she looked at me. "They just vanished. I wish I had answers."

"People can't just all vanish like that; scientific improbability," I said. I hoped she wouldn't think me a jerk for making light of the situation, especially when I couldn't understand what was going on either.

Mei smiled. It only lasted a moment. It looked better than the look of horror on her face when the flames reached the ceiling in the science lab. Still, this hadn't been in my scenarios of what might happen tonight. I had thought the worst case was not seeing Mei at all. Best case, I would finally ask her out and she would say yes. Then there were the other nine-hundred scenarios in between, but not one of them involved everyone vanishing like in some science fiction movie.

"Must be some kind of illusion, right?" I asked.

"Not one I've seen before and I come every year," Mei replied.

Something shuffled. The hair on the back of my neck stood to attention, and I shivered. The noise approached from behind and my fingers curled into a fist. I swallowed the excess saliva and tried to take a deep breath. I glanced at Mei only to find her gaze on me. I had to be the brave one, right? If I ran off, then that would definitely ruin any chance I had. Of course, all of that was dependent on this being real. One of us had to turn around. Right? It should be me, right?

I exhaled and turned with my fist ready. *Who am I kidding? I've never hit anyone in my life, not even hit my pillow in anger.* My heart raced. I glanced to locate the source of the noise.

Shuffle, shuffle.

My mouth felt dry, but I swallowed again. *Where is the noise coming from?* Trees. Grass. Path. Sky.

Shuffle, shuffle.

Trees. My head moved forward as my eyes squinted at the nearest group of trees. Mei's sleeve brushed against mine. I assumed she turned around. She probably figured it was safe to look, since I hadn't screamed and ran for the city streets. My gaze remained focus on the darkness.

From the shadows, a figure emerged. The body hunched over, but the clothing seemed familiar. Across the grass and onto the nearby path. The moon behind them keeping their identity concealed.

Shuffle, shuffle.

The figured raised its head. Miki's grandmother looked our way. I wouldn't exactly say she had a smile on her face, but at least it wasn't a grim reaper like my mind had conjured seconds before. Next movie night with Jace, I would not go with horror.

"Ying Yue?" Mei sounded surprised and stepped forward.

"Expecting someone else?" she replied.

"I thought she didn't speak English?" I whispered to Mei.

Mei turned to me and shrugged as Ying Yue paused in front of us.

"Young man, if you have something to say, say it. Something to ask, you ask it. In answer to your question, I don't speak much English, but anything is possible in this world. Surely you don't expect me to explain every little detail?"

"Yeah, but you said…"

"*This* world? Where did everyone go?" Mei asked.

"Oh, they are still all around us. You just can't see or hear them, but I assure you they are there." Ying Yue raised her finger towards me. "I wasn't sure if you would drink the elixir, but you will thank me one day."

"I don't understand what's going on. I mean—"

"I sense that you both overthink things. That's the problem, you know. So busy thinking about the right words to say, the right things to do, so busy thinking that you never *do* anything. So, I've given you both a chance to do."

I shifted my weight to my left foot and buried my hands in my pockets.

34

"I don't know what game you're playing, but we want to go back now; no tricks," I said.

"Oh, you can go back. At least, you can go back as soon as you finish this little journey, but of course you only have two hours because after that the gateway will close and then you'll be stuck with just each other for company for a very long time."

"But Ying Yue—"

"No buts Mei. You will need to work together to solve nine riddles. Tonight, Chang'e will watch over you both. The lanterns will guide you back, but mind the time. Just two hours, remember?"

"What riddles?" Mei asked.

"Oh dear, I nearly forgot." Ying Yue waved her hand and a piece of paper appeared in front of her. It floated towards Mei, who reached out and grabbed it. "Now I have places to be and things to do. Have fun."

The old lady smiled. It looked as if she bent over to pick something up, but her frame shrunk until a white rabbit sat before us. Its nose twitched a few times before it bounded off towards a nearby tree and vanished into the darkness of the shadows.

"You sure that was just lemonade in the bottle?" I asked.

"Depends. Did you just see this appear out of nowhere and float to me and then her turn into a fluffy little rabbit?"

"I did, and for some reason I find that scarier than if only one of us saw it."

"Agreed," Mei said.

Mei sighed and turned the folded paper over in her hand. I wondered what that had in store for us. Would some kind of dragon appear from it? Would night turn into day? I watched as Mei unfolded the paper. No mythical creatures materialised, but writing covered the paper. I stepped closer to her to read the writing on the paper.

"It's a riddle," Mei said. She looked up at me. "It's a thing we do. We write riddles and then attach them to lanterns. Lao Lao, my grandma, she used to send me one every year from China."

"I follow you wherever you go, but I never miss home. I am not afraid of fire or ice, and I never crave food or thirst. When the light fades, I vanish with it. What am I?" My hand escaped my pocket, and I ran my fingers through my hair. Puzzles I didn't mind, but riddles, riddles I hated. "So, we need to do what? Figure out whatever it is and…"

"I'm assuming if we solve it, we will find the next riddle."

"And if we don't solve it, then we are going to be trapped wherever here is forever. If this is real. I mean, maybe we're really asleep and this is just a really vivid nightmare…" I glanced at Mei. "Sorry, it's not being here with you is a nightmare… I mean like, it's just…"

"It's okay, I know what you mean. Dream, nightmare, hallucination, whatever this is, I think we have no choice but to play along at the moment."

"Fine by me. So, first we answer this riddle, then eight more and everything is back to normal." I tried to sound confident. I probably failed.

I used to love the riddles Lao Lao sent me, but now they didn't seem so fun. My gaze went back to where Ying Yue had stood only moments before. The rabbit, a white rabbit. It was the Mid-Autumn Festival, but the story of Chang'e was just a story. Wasn't it?

"Mei?"

Kane's voice pulled me from my thoughts. I turned to look up at him.

"Sorry, I was just thinking about how she changed to a rabbit and the festival. Never mind me. So maybe if we pick bits of the riddle, we can work out the answer."

"I guess the key is which bit?" Kane said. "Let me read it again."

We both read through the riddle. I watched the paper it in my hands even after I was sure Kane had finished.

39

"When light fades, it vanishes. What do we only see during the day?" Kane asked.

My gaze moved back to the sky. The sun vanished, but technically it was the light rather than something that didn't exist without it. My fingers curled around the cuff of my jumper and I tugged at the sleeves. Ma hated the way it stretched one side of the sleeve, but I continued to do it. The surrounding park looked so much larger now without the people sitting on the grass and walking along the path.

The night sky meant the yellow blossoms on the golden wattle trees were highlighted only by the moonlight. I knew the River Torrens was off to the side, so focused instead on the patch of trees. Maybe I could get lucky and the answer would come to me.

Under one of the larger trees, I saw light, movement... I saw something.

"Can you see that?" I asked.

"What?" Kane asked.

I raised my hand and pointed my finger in the direction of the tree. Moonlight reached the top and some of the outer branches, but a light definitely seemed to glow closer to the trunk.

"Light, a light," I mumbled. "When light disappears. Oh, of course, that makes sense."

"Huh?"

"Light. When light shines on objects, it casts a shadow. But if there is no light, there is no shadow. It doesn't eat or drink."

"Oh, I see. So, what do we do once we've solved it?"

"I guess we go over there where I can see something in the shadow of the tree."

"You're right and that's the only weird glowy thing coming from beneath any as well. Shall we investigate?"

"Race you."

Before I finished the sentence, I started to run across the grass. I felt the blades flick against my ankle as the trees began to fill my view. Kane caught up fast and soon overtook me. Dirt flew from his shoes as he skidded to a stop beneath the tree. He turned to me with a red face and waited until I caught up.

I paused and took a couple of deep breaths before I stepped past Kane. A small bamboo lantern hung from a low branch. Red rice paper covered the frame and a black moon had been painted in ink on one side. Light flickered inside of the lantern and cast shadows on the patches of grass at my feet. Kane stepped up beside me and the soft light lit up his features. I felt

41

the warmth spread in my cheeks and turned back to the lantern.

"Shadows," he said.

The lantern vanished as soon as Kane said the words. A spray of red and gold dust floated to the ground along with a small piece of paper. I reached out to grab it and my head connected with Kane's shoulder.

"Sorry," he said. "Are you alright?"

"Lao Lao says I have a hard head; I'm sure I'll live." I smiled to convince him that the pain I felt in my temple wasn't that bad.

"You sure?"

I nodded. He reached down and picked up the paper from the grass.

"Another riddle."

"It's a deng mi," I murmured. Not a surprise, really.

"A what?"

I turned to look at Kane. "Oh, it's a lantern riddle. Usually, the riddles are written on pieces of paper and attached to the bottom of the lanterns. Always happens during the Mid-Autumn festivals."

"So, they're traditional then?"

I nodded. "For a long time. There is a book written by Zhou Mi and it mentions in it how people would attach riddles to lanterns and that was…" I tried to remember how old it was. "I think it was sometime in the 13th century, but don't quote me on that."

"That's really neat that it's still being done so many hundreds of years later." He looked down at the piece of paper. "Another riddle then."

"As we knew there would be. What does it say?" I asked.

"Um. Twin brothers are tall and sturdy as they work together. They venture only near solids. Who are they?"

"Who, or maybe what?" I said. "I swear I've heard this one before." I didn't want to say it was an easy one.

Kane turned and looked back towards the stalls. "I have an idea, but it seems too obvious. Like the shadow was a little obscure."

"You'll never know unless you say what you think."

"Chopsticks."

I nodded, and he smiled at me.

His head tilted to the side. "You already knew that, didn't you?"

I shrugged. "Maybe."

"That's why I like you. You're smart but not full of yourself. You can have just you knew, like it's not going to change what I think about… Anyway, let's head towards the food and see what we can find."

I wondered what the sentence would have been if he had finished it. *He actually likes me. That's a good start. But what was the end of that thought? Change what he thinks about me? What he thinks about the task? The weirdness of the night? If only he had finished what he started to say.* Still, I would have plenty of time to go over that thought later tonight, and tomorrow, and next week. Lao Lao wasn't wrong when she said I over-analyse stuff.

The smell of food lingered in the air, which seemed odd considering there were no people about. No matter how much I squinted, I couldn't work out from the distance if the stalls still had food.

As we got closer, it became clear the food existed. I breathed in the aroma and my stomach didn't miss a beat. The roasted duck smelt so divine, but I resisted the urge to locate it. The stall to my right had plenty of fruit, and I grabbed a pear from the basket.

My feet stilled, as did the pear just millimetres from my lips. *There were no people, so did it count as stealing?* I glanced towards Kane, who had continued to walk. Maybe he sensed I had paused as he looked over his shoulder.

"Oh, that pear looks good. All these food smells... Like I wasn't that hungry before and now I could just eat all the food." Kane walked back towards me and perused the table.

My mind hadn't yet conceded to the debate about stealing. Kane clearly didn't have any concerns as when he turned back my way, his pear had a bite missing.

"These are good. Go on, eat it."

Kane took another bite. I could always leave a little something... I reached into my jeans and pulled out my wallet, leaving some change in the basket.

"Honest, even in a world of our own," Kane commented.

But at least I felt okay about eating it. Kane hadn't been wrong; the pears were just the right blend of crunchy and juicy. After throwing the stem into a nearby bin, I wiped my mouth on my sleeve. *Oh well.*

"I wonder why they have so many pears. There must be ten times the pears here compared to the other fruit."

"During the Mid-Autumn Festival, pears are eaten to attempt and avoid being parted with someone all of a sudden. It's why you can't share a pear during it. Mooncakes though, everyone shares them."

Jace probably wouldn't." Kane turned on the spot. "Right, so now we have energy we need to locate the chopsticks. So, some kind of hot food stall, yes?"

"I think that sounds more probable. There are probably several though that sell foods requiring the utensils, though." I sighed.

"You okay?"

I tucked my hair behind my ear and shrugged as my own words haunted me. *Several? Dozens? Would all the stalls be in the same area? Somewhere else?* The cheery red lanterns that hung on strings over our heads didn't lift my mood.

"Mei?"

"Just overwhelmed, I think. Limited time, no clue if we are looking in the right spot. I don't know, I just want to go home."

Kane stepped closer. "Yeah, me too; the quicker we find these twins, the better than. Am I right?" he exaggerated his enthusiasm as he said it.

A smile crossed my lips, and I nodded.

"Let's approach this scientifically. We need a quick plan."

"I don't know, maybe..." I tried to think of something logical. "I'll go along that side there; you go behind to make sure it's not hiding under the tables. Perhaps if we keep saying 'chopsticks', the lantern will appear."

"I like it. Good plan."

He just nodded and hurried to where I had indicated. We moved parallel, calling out 'chopsticks' like we had lost our pet dog.

"Mei, it's there!" Kane exclaimed.

I looked up from the table in time to see Kane run towards a stall with noodle stir-fries. My stomach growled, but it would have to wait. I ran over to the stand just as a red lantern floated up from behind the main serving table. Kane reached out and caught the side of it and it vanished into the same dust as before.

"Definitely chopsticks," Kane said.

"And another riddle."

I picked up the piece of paper that had floated onto the table.

"I'm glad you're here with me. Together, I am sure we can do this," Kane said.

I bit my bottom lip for a moment. *Time to be brave, Mei.* "I'm glad you're here too."

When I managed to look his way, our gaze locked for just a moment. He smiled. I smiled. *Good job, Mei.*

48

Chapter 6

Kane

Two riddles solved already. I checked my watch. So far, we had plenty of time to finish the quest well within the time. Of course, if the riddles were trickier than the first, then we might be in trouble.

Mei held the piece of paper in her hand and I leaned closer to read it.

"This lovely maiden loves to eat leaves but will never touch meat. She works each day, spinning and weaving for others. Who is she?" Mei said.

I ran my hand through my hair.

"Maiden? So, it must be a girl?" I ventured.

"Maybe. The spinning and weaving part I'm not so sure about." Mei looked up at me. "I hear spinning and I think of spiders."

I shivered. Spiders were not my favourite creature. "What else spins? A dancer? Can a dancer weave?"

"There were dancers in the parade earlier." Mei's hand moved back and forth in front of her body. "I guess when they dance, they weave, right?"

"Yeah, but not all the dancers were girls and we have no idea about their food preferences."

"Oh, good point. Guess we have to think a little more about this one."

She sounded far more confident than I felt as she bit her lip. Mei turned to look behind us. The way the light fell on her face made my heart pound. She looked even prettier in the moonlight than across the classroom in the middle of the day. I cast my gaze back to the ground in case she noticed. With a sigh, I shoved my hands back into my jean pockets.

"Maybe we could just walk around. Maybe we might see something?" *Or maybe she'll think I can't construct a proper sentence.*

"Sure, good idea."

I let the breath I had held go, and we walked through the remainder of the food stalls until we started seeing others. My gaze fell on the little bottles of sparkling liquid as we passed them by. I almost expected Ying Yue to appear and tell us that we were April fools, but of course, it wasn't April, and I didn't consider myself a fool most of the time.

Mei's steps silenced beside me, and I stopped as well. When I looked over my shoulder, her attention seemed focused on the stall beside her, with purses and hair ties and other girly things. I hesitated to step up beside her. As much as I hated to admit it, I didn't want to be caught looking at girly things.

"Should we keep looking around?" I asked.

"Huh?" Mei turned to look at me. "Oh, sorry. These items, what do they have in common?"

Dare I say it?

"Err, they all look... they all look..."

Mei inclined her head, and I saw the corners of her mouth twitch before she raised her hand. I had no doubt she had a smile hidden behind her hands. I sighed.

"It's all stuff my mum would prefer to look at than me."

Her eyebrows arched. Mei lowered her hands, and I saw the suspected smile.

"Yeah, I don't imagine my father racing to this stall first. Besides the fact that this table has more female oriented goods, there is something else that they have in common."

"There is?" I stepped forward and took another look at the contents of the table.

"A lot are pink."

Mei's laughter echoed around us. "True, but look closer. Think about home ec class."

I turned to look at her. "I would rather not remember the horrors of home ec class." My mind conjured the image of Jessie Delaney who sewed over her finger on the sewing machine while making the pencil case. Cold chills ran down my spine.

"What did we use, though?"

"Use? Um, equipment, cotton, material..."

"Exactly!"

"All these items are not just made from material; they're made from a specific type of material."

"They are?" My gaze moved over the items. They shone a little, like the fancy dresses the girls wore to the formals or graduation night.

"Shiny material?"

"Close enough. It's silk."

"And silk comes from silkworms that don't eat meat."

"And who spends her days spinning for others?"

"I read once somewhere that the poor things have to die to get the silk," I said.

"Mostly, but there is ahimsa silk."

"Never heard of it."

"Neither had I until Lao Lao told me. She likes to read a lot. A man in India has this process where the silkworms don't die in the process."

"I kind of like the idea of them not having to die. Imagine doing all that work just to die and have someone make money from it. I don't know, doesn't seem fair to me."

"Me neither."

Mei picked up one of the purses and stroked her finger on the material. I waited to see a lantern appear with a clue, but nothing. My gaze fell to the ground in case a little white rabbit lurked somewhere.

"Let's say the answer is silk or silkworms. Where's the next clue?"

"Maybe it's the right answer, but the wrong stall?" Mei suggested.

"Fabric stall, maybe?" I hadn't noticed anything vaguely like that when I had looked around with Jace. Then again, we'd been caught up in the food area, mostly.

Mei placed the purse back on the table and I stepped back to give her room. I waved my hand in the direction of the stalls that spread out in front of us. I doubted we would head to where the food was.

"I think it will be over that way. If they have fabric, then they would want it under cover," Mei said.

I moved my gaze in the direction she started to walk. Beyond the surrounding tables, there appeared to be a row of white tents extending back towards the fence. I did a jog and fell into step beside her.

We entered the little dirt laneway with stalls in white tents on either side. I felt Mei's hand brush against mine. *Should I move further away?* I glanced at her from the corner of my eye, but her attention wasn't on me. *Probably overthinking it.*

So many stalls selling all manner of things, but most had things that they wouldn't want to get wet. My gaze passed over each one as we walked past. I wasn't entirely sure what the fabric should look like. Mum often bought these big rolls of fabrics but I couldn't see them wanting to bring that to a festival.

Mei's hand pressed against mine for a moment as she said, "Over there."

When I looked to the side, I saw a table inside one tent covered in different colours of what I assumed was silk fabric. It was shiny and the prices I could see displayed made me twitch; with what I earned after school, I would be lucky to be able to afford a tiny ribbon.

"Oh, they're all so beautiful," Mei said.

She walked to the table and ran her hand over a few pieces. "Repeat the riddle for me, please, Kane."

"Um, this lovely maiden loves to eat leaves but will never touch meat. Each day she works spinning and weaving for others." That was the best I could remember, since Mei had the riddle in her pocket.

"It has to be here. Who's going to say it?" Mei asked.

"You worked it out, so you should have the honour."

Mei smiled. "She is a silkworm."

A red lantern floated from beneath the table. Mei reached for it, but it slipped through her fingers as it rose. I moved forward and caught the riddle hanging from it. Not only did I see the spray of red and gold dust, but I looked away as it fell on me. When I opened my eyes, I breathed with relief that I didn't sparkle.

"Okay, time for the next one then!"

Chapter 7
Mei

"When you cry, she cries. When you laugh, she laughs. You can ask who she is, but it's up to you to hear her reply," I said.

Unlike the other riddles we had solved, this one had a special detail. In one of the corners of the paper, a little figure eight had been made with ink. I doubted it would be anything accidental, since everything so far had been planned in detail to suit where we were. That little squiggle meant something; I just wasn't sure what.

"Eight. Eight what?" Kane said. "Jace would say eight serves, but I don't know who would cry over that."

I smiled. "Depends who had to clean up the results on the ground. Though I don't think I would cry, another strong reaction comes to mind."

"So, eight..." Kane started to click his tongue. My father had the same habit when he attempted to solve any maths calculation.

"Maybe stall number eight?" I suggested.

"Oh, I think I still have the map thingy I got when we got here."

Kane reached into his pocket and pulled out a wrinkled, but neatly folded, piece of paper. I watched as he tugged at one corner of the paper once, twice, three times before the paper relented and unfolded.

"That's the main gate there," he said, and pointed to the section beside the tram tracks.

I stepped forward, so I stood beside him. My hair fell over my shoulder as I studied the map trying to locate stall eight. My finger traced along the squares with numbers inside.

"Why aren't the numbers in a more logical order?" Kane grumbled.

He had a point. I'm sure the organisation had made sense to someone, but at that point trying to locate one number was like finding a needle. My gaze moved to my wrist, and I checked the time. Thirty minutes had already lapsed, and it seemed we still had several more to solve.

"There it is." Kane released the paper on my side to tap his finger on one section.

Sure enough, a stall number eight was labelled as being behind the stage. My shoulders drooped as I realised that meant going back to where we had found the first lantern under the tree. If we had to keep covering so much ground, I worried if we would find and solve all the riddles in time.

"Hey, don't worry Mei. We're doing okay so far," Kane said softly. "We'll head over there and check it out. We make a good team. We got this."

I tried to look at enthusiastic and confident as he sounded. He reached out and grabbed my hand and nodded towards where we had to go. A smile crossed my face and together we started to jog in that direction. His hand felt warm holding mine, and I worried he would notice the sweat on my hands.

Stall eight was wedged between a table with paper lanterns and another selling miniature paintings of moonscapes. They were rather pretty, and I wished I had seen them earlier when Lucy and I arrived. Lao Lao would love the one of the moon with the rabbit silhouette. If we made it back, I would definitely go and get that for her.

"I don't see anything on this stall that is about a girl crying," Kane said.

Neither did I. Dolls dressed in different coloured hanfu and cheongsam lined the table. One of them could be those dolls that cry, though. When I was six, I had wanted one so badly, but Ma had said no.

"The riddle said, When you cry, she cries. When you laugh, she laughs. Is there maybe a doll on here that records what you say and plays it back?"

"Oh man, I remember a girl in kindy had one of them. You remember? It had her voice on like four of the messages and then she'd recorded her mother swearing."

"Last time Sia was allowed to bring the doll to kindy, ever." I laughed at it. Although that incident had been the sole reason Ma had said no. Not that I had ever heard her swear, not in English anyway, but she didn't like the idea of it recording me.

"How would we know if they talk?" Kane asked.

I shrugged. "I guess we check each one?"

Which is what we did. Kane started at one end of the table and me at the other. I picked up each doll to check if they were hard plastic first and if they were, peeked on the back of it to see if there was a sound box. My mind was conscious of the time and I forced myself to stop looking at the watch.

"I'm not finding anything," Kane said.

I shook my head. He wasn't the only one.

"I don't think this is the right place. I'm sure the lantern would have appeared by now if it were."

"So, we've stuffed something up with the riddle, then."

He pulled out the piece of paper and read it aloud again.

"You know it vaguely reminds me of something, but I just can't think of what exactly," Kane said.

"It could be an infinity symbol," I suggested. It didn't seem likely, but given the clue.

"I've got it! We were thinking about this all wrong! Doesn't it remind you of that sculpture in Rundle Mall? You know, the one with the two balls?"

"But what would that have to do with the riddle? Shouldn't all the answers be here at the festival?"

"I don't know where they should be, but think about it. It has the same shape. Maybe that's what we are supposed to be looking for."

"Kane, if it's wrong, we will lose a lot of time getting there and back," I said.

"But we're getting nowhere here. Come on, if we hurry, it shouldn't take long. Besides, without the traffic and people to slow us down, we can do it," Kane said.

"Okay, which way should we go? I don't come into the city much except with family."

Kane turned on the spot. "That way. If we go straight down King William Road, then we can't really get lost. Come on."

He waved at me and we started to jog down the makeshift pathways towards the entrance. The tram tracks were empty, and no cars were on the road as we turned right and started running down the footpath. Kane managed to stay just ahead of me, which I appreciated since I only had a vague idea where we were going. The Adelaide Festival Centre and Hyde Park were soon behind us as we came up to a large intersection.

Kane paused at the corner and waited for me to catch up. "We can cross over to the other side. This is North Terrace, so it's the next block down. Come on."

He was right. We crossed the intersection, and the shops passed by in a blur as I saw the sign ahead for Rundle Mall. At least I knew where we were now. Kane turned left into the mall and I followed. The Malls Balls were a fair way down and our steps echoed around. The empty shops with their lights on made my skin crawl, like some kind of horror movie where the population had been wiped out and the remaining survivors were being hunted.

"I see them!" Kane yelled and his pace slowed.

I grabbed my waist as the stitch started to pinch and slowed down as well. The gigantic silver balls loomed in front of us as we both came to a stop.

"I think you might have been right. Look up Kane."

The shiny silver metal surface of the sculpture was lit by the shop lights on either side of the mall. Our own reflections stared back at us, though we looked a bit distorted.

"When you cry, she cries," Kane muttered, a small smile formed on his lips as he turned to me.

"When you laugh, she laughs," I added.

The riddle, it was about something copying, but not necessarily a girl.

"It's a mirror. The entire ball is a mirror, and it reflects your emotions or actions or speech. We control it!" Kane said.

A lantern floated from behind the sculpture and towards us. I reached out to grab it and it vanished. Kane caught the paper note that appeared as the red and gold dust fell to the ground.

"Okay, ready for the next one?" he asked.

I nodded.

64

Chapter 8
Kane

"Why is the library the tallest building?" I said. "Huh? I mean, it's not. Well, I mean, I'm guessing they're talking about the city library?"

"We passed it back there," Mei said and turned to point back the way we had come.

I don't think I'd ever set forth in the city library before. The high school library for sure and the one close by home, but I'd never had a reason to come into the city.

Mei reached out for the note and I released my hold on it. I straightened up and took a couple of deep breaths. If tonight had taught me anything, it was that I should get off my butt and go for a walk more.

"I guess we head there and hope it will make sense?"

Mei folded the note and put it in her pocket. A breeze passed around us and I saw Mei tug on the ends of her jumper.

"Cold?" I asked.

"Oh, I'm okay. I think the sudden rush from running and now standing still... Just a chill, I guess." She smiled, though. A nice smile. "It's not much of a riddle detail-wise, is it? All the others had more to go by."

"Let's hope that means that it's an easy one for us to solve."

"Since the library is the only thing we have to go by, we need to decide which one. The State Library is further away, but the city library is just down there."

"I wonder if it matters. I mean, it's talking about libraries as a collective. So, something they all have in common. I think the one closest makes more sense."

"I agree, plus that also is leading us back towards the park and I have a feeling that's where this will all hopefully end."

"Good point."

Mei took the lead since I only had a vague idea of where we were going. She seemed way more confident with the way she walked with ease. I tried to focus on the path ahead, but the breeze sent waves of her scent my way.

We reached the deserted library. Despite the lights being on, I hesitated to enter it. Surely, they wouldn't have put a clue in there, right?

"There's nothing outside I can see to answer it. It's not the tallest."

"Short riddles appear to be more difficult than the wordy ones. I don't know if we should try the door."

"Feels like we are thinking of breaking into the library," Mei said.

"I'm not sure that is possible. I mean, if the door opens, then technically, we're not breaking in... just entering," I said. My thoughts went to what my parents would say if they found out. My brother crashing the car had been bad enough, but what if I got caught for a break and enter? They would ground me until... well, forever.

Mei reached out her hand towards the door. Her hand hovered; her feet didn't step any closer. To enter or not to enter; that was the dilemma.

"There are no people, so no one to tell," I said.

"They have cameras though," Mei said, and pointed through the window.

I glanced into the library and saw the camera.

"You reckon they work? I mean, considering everything? I don't think there's much we can do. If the answer is in there, we have to be there as well. If we get caught, just blame me. Plus, if the doors open, then technically, they let us in." I tried to sound more confident than I felt.

My feet stepped closer to the door and Mei's hand fell away as the doors automatically opened. After a moment's pause to relish what could be my last night of freedom, I stepped inside. We walked up the stairs to the third floor since I didn't want to look around for a lift, since the thought of being trapped in one forever didn't thrill me.

The stairs curled around and no matter how hard I tried to be quiet, Mei and I sounded like elephants walking on bubble wrap. Once we reached the library, we stopped. I had no idea where to start or go or what to do.

"Okay, so we think it's more about a library than this specific one. Maybe one of the ancient ones?" Mei suggested. "I'm going to head that way and see if there's something in the non-fiction or reference sections."

I felt I should have a suggestion of my own, but I had nothing. My gaze moved around the unfamiliar surrounding before I forced my hands into my jeans pockets as far as I could. I followed Mei until she came to a stop. Her hand ran along the spines of books on one shelf before she stopped to wiggle one book from its position.

As Mei sat on the vinyl floor, I glanced around at the empty tables with chairs pushed neatly under them. Back home, were people sitting at those desks? Browsing the shelves for a book they wanted? Maybe even sitting on the seats sending text messages? I glanced at my watch; probably not. The library would have closed by now.

"That's a point," I said.

"What is?" Mei asked.

"The library would normally be closed by now. So, since it was open, there must be a reason, like the answer in here."

"Perhaps we should just try something random like: is it the library?" Mei said.

I looked around and hoped to see a lantern float from somewhere. Nothing appeared.

"I don't the answer could be that. It asks why it's the tallest. Obviously not because of actual height, so tallest as in what?" I said to myself. "You think more out of the box than I do, Mei. Why is the library the tallest building?"

"It just doesn't make sense," she whispered.

"None of this makes any sense," I said. My voice sounded much louder than I intended, and I cringed. No librarian appeared to tell me to be quiet. *Why do I still feel guilty?*

"Here I was thinking Ying Yue was just like my lao lao. I mean, I thought magic was just something for stories, but all this is just a whole other level of scientific thinking and possibilities."

"When we make it back home, like back where there are people, I kinda wonder if we are even going to remember all this? I mean, will we just open our eyes and think it was all some weird dream?"

"That would be a shame, then."

I looked up as Mei turned to smile at me. Words failed me and I smiled back.

At this point, it seemed the answer wasn't going to be found amongst the library shelves or under the tables. I moved over to one of the windows and looked outside before I turned back to look at all the shelves and the books...

"Oh no, surely that's not the answer. It can't be," I murmured.

Mei looked up from the book in her hand. "Do you have it?"

"I don't know. It's kind of childish, or like a bad dad joke." I paused and ran my hand through my hair. "What's all around us, Mei?"

"Books mainly."

"And what are books?"

"Information?"

"Yeah, that, but think more fiction. What are they?"

"Entertaining? They're each a —" Mei paused and shook her head. "No, surely it isn't that?"

"Only one way to find out." I nodded and my face contorted at how stupid I was about to sound, even if it was right. "The library is the tallest building because it has the most stories."

Chapter 9
Mei

A lantern squeezed out from the space on the shelf where I had removed the books. I pushed the books aside in front of me and crawled towards it. My fingers closed on the piece of paper and the lantern vanished. A sprinkle of gold and red dust fell around me.

"I am totally going to tell my dad that one for Father's Day next year," Kane said.

I turned my head in time to see him crouch beside me.

"Mine too. He'll think it's the funniest thing ever. Meanwhile, here we are at the moment breathing a sigh of relief that it was the correct answer."

"Upside is that we are officially halfway through this riddle challenge, Mei."

"We are. We make a great team."

"We do," he replied. "We should do this again. Like, not the whole riddle hunt or be trapped forever thing. You know, maybe watch a movie or something."

My lips curved into a smile. "I'd like that."

Kane smiled back at me. I felt shy as he looked my way and looked back at the paper in my hand.

"So, what does the note say this time?" Kane asked.

"It works hard all its life; it counts number day and night but can never get back past twelve. What is it?" I read.

Somewhere in the room, I heard the rhythmic tick-tock of the clock. The clock seemed like the obvious answer.

"I know what it is," I said.

"Already?"

"A clock works day and night and doesn't get past twelve."

"A digital clock does. I mean, it goes up to twenty-three technically."

"Oh, I didn't think of that."

"You're probably right, though. I mean, you said these riddles date way back in history, so I'm pretty certain they only had the basic twelve-hour clock. It's a clock," Kane said.

He turned on the spot. The clock continued to work without missing a beat. I glanced around but saw no lantern.

"Let's assume it is a clock, because it makes sense and I can't think of anything else it might be. We will probably end up back at the park, right?"

Kane nodded. "I would assume this will end where it started. Are you thinking about the clock that's near the park?"

"I am."

"We better get moving then."

We hurried to the stairs. Neither of us seemed as concerned about being caught as our footsteps echoed in the small space. Once we reached the ground floor, we left through the same doors we had entered.

"Back that way," Kane said.

The warm air surrounded us as the automatic doors closed behind us. I nodded in response to the direction and we began to walk back down Rundle Mall.

"It's so weird without all the people. Like, this is how it is most nights, I guess... well, maybe a few who have had too many wandering about. I don't know, it's like a ghost town, isn't it?"

"I remember the year seven camp where we went down to the Murray River camp. I found that very eerie. Most of the time I had been worried a shui gui would appear," I said. The memory brought a smile to my face now, but a few years ago, that had given me nightmares. Lao Lao had been told off by Ma for telling me such stories just nights before the camp.

"What's a shay-grey?

The giggle escaped before I had a chance. "Sorry, you were close. It has a *sh* sound at the beginning. They both sort of rhyme with bay. Shui gui."

Kane tried again with better success. Not perfect, but most would understand what he meant. "So, what is a shui gui then?"

"It's like a water ghost. So, according to what I remember my lao lao telling me, they are like a ghost spirit or soul that lives in water where they drowned. They lurk there under the water's surface, waiting to grab hold of a living person and drag them beneath the surface. Once there, they go through a ti shen - so a process where they take over the living body and trap that other spirit in the water. So, the whole thing repeats as the new shui gui will seek a victim in order to do the same thing."

"That is both fascinating and slightly disturbing at the same time."

I nodded. "I think what made it worse was the water in the Murray is so murky. You can't see a thing that could be lurking just below the surface. I was so pleased for that camp to be over and to come home."

"All I remember from that trip was going out in those kayak things and yeah, the water was pretty murky. I don't think I'll look at water the same way again."

"I thought you liked horror movies," I said.

Whoops, probably gave away that I knew a little too much there. If it wouldn't have been obvious, I would have kicked myself right there, but instead I allowed the embarrassment to show on my face. *At least I can blame any flush on the warm air and exercise. Yep, that would work.*

"I like different movies, but movies are one thing. I don't know, I find those legends and folktales are like a bit closer to reality. Like so many cultures have similar stories that you have to wonder if the reason for that is that they're real."

"True. My ma said that if we believed in everything though, we would be too afraid to live. So, it is best to focus on what you can see and do something about."

"Sounds like a smart mum."

I felt his hand brush against mine. *Why can I talk about anything except my own feelings?* Then his fingers curled around mine. My feet halted, but my heart raced. I looked up at him to see him nod to the side.

"We need to turn here," he said.

"Oh, yeah. Sorry, was just thinking."

We turned the corner and continued back towards the park. I could have pulled back on my hand. I could have asked him to let it go. I could have, but I didn't because I liked it.

"I guess we were lucky," Kane said.

"How so?"

"Well, out of all the people we could have ended up with here, I think we lucked out. Well, I think I did, because you know, you're smart and know stuff I don't…"

"There are things you know that I don't too. Perhaps Ying Yue has some ultimate plan in store for us."

"Do you think she did this to lots, or just us?" Kane asked. "Like do you think there are hundreds of these empty Adelaide clones at this moment, with people searching for answers to riddles?"

"I don't know. I hadn't thought about it. Part of me still thinks this isn't real, but I don't know. I mean, I don't think Miki's grandmother is… It sounds silly to say supernatural, but you know. Oh, I don't understand any of it."

"Maybe she is some super-tech whizz, and this is all like some super high-definition virtual reality game that we are testing for her."

I shook my head as our laughter echoed through the empty streets. I could see the lights from the park welcoming our return as we crossed the final intersection. There, at the entrance, a clock had been placed.

"Here we go, let's say it," Kane said.

"Clock," we said.

A lantern floated out from behind the sandbags that weighted the stand in place. Kane grabbed the seventh note as the lantern became red and gold dust that glittered and disappeared before it reached the ground.

"That's another thing," Kane said.

"What?"

"Where do the lanterns go? Like when they go that thing, do they still exist or not exist?"

"And did they exist to begin with?" I added.

"I swear this is harder than a day at school," Kane said.

He released my hand and unfolded the piece of paper. We were about to know what riddle we needed to solve next.

I angled the note under the light to better see the words. "He devotes his life to watching the house while his mate follows the master wherever he goes. A gentleman sees him and turns away. A villain sees him and it spells bad luck. Who is he?"

"So, there are two objects I'm guessing that get separated?" Mei said.

I nodded. "Sounds like it."

"Okay, now I'm not a fan of this riddle at all."

Her nose twitched as she glowered at the note. She looked so annoyed. "Hey, why are you laughing? This is the hardest one we've had yet, in my opinion."

"Ah, just your reaction. I don't think I've seen you look so annoyed before," I replied.

Mei's shoulders relaxed, and she sighed.

"We're almost done with all of this," I said to keep the mood positive. I had actually managed to hold her hand, and she didn't pull it away or object or anything. One wrong comment though, and I feared I would stuff up the progress I'd made so far. "We know we are in the right place. I don't think we'll have to head into the city again. It's almost like we've done a circle."

"Huh, we started there and went there, there…" Mei said as she turned and pointed in the direction of where each riddle had been found so far. "You're right, a wonky circle, but yeah."

"I bet it means something."

"Probably, but we'd better focus on this, especially with time ticking."

Mei wasn't wrong about that. We didn't have long to go. Sure, we only had a couple of riddles left, but I had no idea about this one.

"Let's continue looking in a circular mode. Who knows, maybe as we walk around, something will click," I said.

"Well, the circle would continue over there-ish." Mei pointed over my shoulder.

"Next time I have to calculate a circumference, I'm going to be haunted by this. Oh wait, not haunted. Enough of the ghost tales for tonight."

"We know it is about two, a pair."

"And we know that they don't stay together, so it can't be like the chopsticks that you use at the same time because one without the other is a bit pointless, right?" I added. "What about the bit, 'a villain sees him and it spells bad luck'?"

"Yeah, I wonder about that as well. The master must be an owner, someone they help?"

"So, who helps, but is bad news for crooks?"

"Police come to mind, but they don't follow someone."

"They would if they were in protective custody," I said. I'd heard that one on a TV show. "No, I like the idea, but I don't think it's a person. I think the object thing is right. But what?"

"I remember over there is where the lanterns were being sold. Lucy got us one each before the parade."

"What happened to it?"

Mei looked up at me and shrugged. "A little girl missed out on a moon rabbit one, so I gave her mine. Anyway, it will save me from getting it home in one piece. Hang on."

By the time I realised she had stopped, I had gone several meters. Mei stood there with her hand raised as her index finger tapped the air.

"Two parts that work together but don't stay together. I know what it is. Come on."

She ran and grabbed my hand before I could ask what or where.

"Where are we going?"

"The stall, the one behind the lanterns, had those padlock things. A lock stays home, but the key goes with the owner," Mei said.

"Oh, that makes sense." *Sort of.* "Why would there be padlocks here?"

Mei didn't answer as I saw the stall for myself. Silver and gold padlocks with keys attached to the handle of the locks covered the table. Different shapes and styles. The stall itself had been set up to raise money for a local charity supporting free language lessons to those wanting to learn Mandarin or Cantonese. Not a bad idea if things worked out with Mei to learn a bit more of the language.

"It's a lock," Mei said.

Her feet bounced on the ground as she bit her lip. The smile faded as we waited for a lantern to appear. And waited. No lantern.

"It has to be the right answer. It's the right place. It makes sense…"

"Yeah, I think it is, too. Maybe we haven't done something that we need to. I mean, I've seen these padlocks everywhere on fences, but usually they have like things written on them and stuff." I glanced over the table and my gaze fell on the sign:

Engrave a lock. "I think we need to lock it on that makeshift fence."

"That's all?"

"Maybe?" I looked again at the sign.

My hand felt the warm air as Mei let go. She picked up one of the keys and walked around the table to a fence that already had a few hundred locks on it. I leaned to the side to see her take the key off the lock. Her fingers hooked the lock on and I heard the click.

Still nothing, but I suspected we missed another step. Mei walked back over to me and I saw her wipe her eyes.

"You okay?" I asked.

Her shoulders slumped as she pushed her sleeve up her arm and looked at her watch. "I really thought it would work. We're running out of time, Kane."

"We can do it. Choose another lock."

I reached over the table and grabbed one of the engravers. Three years of metalwork was about to pay off. Mei picked another lock and held it out. I took it off her hand and placed it on the table, gripping the cool metal between my left and right thumb and index finger.

"What should we engrave? Our initials?" I asked.

"Our names? Initials. I saw both over there." Mei pointed to the wall.

The idea of names suited me. I crouched down beside the table that was too low to comfortably engrave the lock. I flicked the button, and the engraver started to hum while my hand started to shake. A deep breath. I put metal on metal and engraved M-E-I and below it the letters K-A-N-E. Most probably put a heart around it, but that might be too soon, even for me. Instead, I engraved a lantern shape around our names with a riddle hanging below it. One flick and the engraver went quiet.

I blew on the padlock to rid it of the tiny bits of metal dust. *Not a bad job.* I passed the padlock to Mei so I could wipe my hands on my jeans. She seemed to look a long while at the lock.

"It's a... it's a deng mi." I hoped I hadn't butchered the pronunciation.

"I know. That's so beautiful. Hang on a second."

Mei reached into her pocket and pulled out her phone. I heard the familiar click.

"Something to remember," she said. "Let's try it again."

We walked to the fence together and Mei took the key off it like she had with the other one. The lock in her hand was ready to be secured when she stopped.

"You do it," Mei said.

"Count of three, I click and you say the magic words. One, two, three."

The lock clicked as Mei shouted, "Lock and key!"

The seventh lantern floated up behind the fence.

"Oh quick, we need to get around the fence before it floats away," I said.

I ran one way while Mei went the other. The red lantern continued to rise. Mei had already gone around the fence, but the lantern seemed to be headed my way. My shoes skidded on the dirt as I reached out to grab the fence to swing myself around.

With the lantern out of Mei's reach, I Jumped onto a wooden picnic table and snatched the lantern just in time. *Why am I always getting covered in the sparkles?* Still no time to grumble as the clue floated down towards the table.

Mei picked it up and waited for me to step down from the table. Mum would kill me if I did that any other time. Once I'd done it at a picnic at Port Adelaide and she had lectured every one of us about how people eat there and to keep our shoes off it. On this occasion, I felt justified.

"Okay, time to read the next one," I said.

Mei handed me the paper, and I started to unfold it. We were almost home.

Chapter 11
Mei

Just two to go. Please let it be an easy one. I crossed my fingers. We needed a little luck, with only twenty minutes to go.

"It can be round like a saucer or curved like a smile. What is it?" Kane read from the note.

"An easy one; thank goodness for that," I said.

"It's the moon, right?"

"Yeah, but since you just said the magic word, and no lantern is attempting to flee, it means a certain moon. Grr, there is no consistency in these riddles. Specific, vague... They should fire whoever wrote these."

"When we get back, you can complain to... I don't know, but I support firing the person responsible."

"Good, okay. We got this," I said and crossed my fingers for good measure.

"We need to find one certain moon at a festival dedicated to the moon? Now that would be just cruel. I guess because the riddle was easy, the locating of it had to be less so. I wonder if there was a business of something with the moon in the title?"

"Worth a look."

Kane pulled out the creased map again and placed it on the table. He used his hand to smooth out the bumps. I ran my gaze down the list of stall holders. A few had the magic word, but it didn't seem to fit.

"What did you say before, Kane? About the festival?"

"Huh?" Kane turned to look at me. His gaze looked skyward for a moment. "Um, I said we had to find a moon at a moon festival. Something like that."

"I don't think it would be any moon. Like this is riddle eight, we have just this and one more to go before we get home. These moons aren't important. At least, they're not important in the big picture."

"True, but we already both looked up at the moon and said it, and we're still waiting for the red and gold glitter."

"In the story about Chang'e, she ascended to the moon as an immortal. Depending on the version because of her love or deception of Hou Yi. The moon is immortal, in a sense, since it's always up there."

"But unlike her, we can't ascend to the moon and back in just over fifteen minutes."

"Can we bring the moon to us?"

"Didn't bring a lasso with me tonight, Mei," Kane said.

A smile formed on my lips; I knew the movie he'd got that idea from. My feet stepped back, and I looked where we had come. If the circle followed, we would end up by the river.

"Penny for your thoughts."

"The circle would say to the river. So, we go there?"

Kane shrugged and nodded. "Let's go."

He held out his hand, and I took it. I couldn't wait to tell Lucy if we ever got back. A few tears tried to escape, but I sniffed and pushed them away. We needed to be positive.

We left the stalls behind and crossed over the grass to the bank of the river. Lanterns bobbed on the surface of the water as the water moved downstream.

"Mei?"

"Yeah?"

"When we get back, I want this to continue. Like not the riddles, but us. You know, like I said, see a movie together or something. Just wanted to say that and be clear. I mean, I would want that anyway. It's not like I said it just because of all this weirdness."

"Me too Kane. Tonight is the start of something for us."

"I've liked you for a while. I mean, you're intelligent, beautiful, and kind. Like giving that kid your lantern. I just feel you deserve the best in the world can offer. And I don't think I'm the best, because that would be a bit, well, you know, full of myself. Ugh, now I'm rambling. It sounded so much better in my head. It's just, if when we go back and all this vanishes and if we don't remember anything... Well, I just want to know that I told you. Did any of that make sense?"

"It made sense. Can I just say ditto because otherwise I'm probably going to ramble as well and make no sense?"

I took a deep breath, but for once I didn't feel the familiar warmth flood my cheeks. Still, I couldn't quite bring myself to look at him. His reflection would have to do.

"Maybe we the moon is already here for us," Kane said.

"How?"

"Because I'm watching your reflection in the river, which means somewhere we should be able to see the moon's reflection, too."

We looked at the surface of the river, but I couldn't see the moon's reflection.

"What about we take a photo?"

I reached into my pocket for the phone and we both took

several steps away from the river. The last thing I wanted was to lose my phone on a magical adventure and explain it to my parents. I snapped a few photos of the moon above and flicked through them.

"This is the best one. You know, I read once that some people were scared to have their photo taken because they thought it would steal their soul away."

"Soul of the moon, maybe? The spirit of Chang'e?" Kane asked.

I took a deep breath. One chance to live, right? And if we remembered none of this, then what would it matter? Those thought spun in my mind as I felt Kane's hand touch my cheek. I turned towards him and looked up. The moonlight played with the colours in his hair and made his eyes shine. His hand fell away, and he stood close beside me as he gave my hand a squeeze.

"Ready?" I asked.

"Ready."

With a smile, we both said, "It's the moon."

I wasn't sure where the lantern rose from. My attention focused on the phone instead. It floated over the water for a while before it came onto the land. It paused near Kane and he reached up to touch it. I expected to see the dust, but instead it headed off behind us.

We both turned and hurried after the red beacon. It weaved around trees with grace while we struggled to catch up with it. The lantern seemed to be on a course somewhere because otherwise it would have floated away or burst into dust.

"Where's it going?" I asked.

"I don't know. It didn't leave us any notes or clues," he answered.

That hadn't happened all night, and I wondered if it had something to do with the fact that it was the last lantern we had to find before we could go home.

"It's heading for the rotunda," Kane said.

I could see the rotunda ahead of us. The lantern hovered in front of it, no higher than my head. There were no musicians in the rotunda, but something else ebbed and whirled inside it. The lantern wouldn't let us pass. We tried to duck under it, go around it, and even ran at it. No matter what we did, the lantern blocked our way.

"If that's the way home, then where is the ninth lantern?" Kane said.

"Wait, look Kane. All those lanterns."

Seven red lanterns floated into an incomplete circle shape to frame the portal home. The red lanterns hovered in contrast to the golden sparkles and swirls of the portal.

Lantern eight came closer and when I touched it, a piece of paper fell from the dust. The lantern then reformed and took its place with the other ones.

"The last one," I said.

"And we've only got two minutes before we run out of time."

"It belongs to you but gets used more by other people," I read from the paper.

I turned it over to see a small moon in the top corner.

"You know what?" Kane said. "It will sound strange, but I think Chang'e herself put these riddles here for us tonight."

"That drink Ying Yue gave us, she insisted, we have those bottles. She didn't insist on choosing one for Lucy. That was the catalyst for everything that's happened. I wonder if Ying Yue and Chang'e are connected somehow?"

"Isn't she supposed to help those who are in love or something?" Kane asked.

I smiled. "There are a lot of stories about her. Maybe she did drink for love after all. So, what do we own and everyone else uses?"

"Pens, money... Nah, has to be more personal for the last clue. Something unique."

"Kane, do you think...?" I spoke.

"Mei, that's probably it."

"Huh?"

"Sorry, I cut you off, but you just said it. Our names. We hardly ever use our own name, but everyone else uses it every day."

Mei looked at her watch. "An easy one, then. We got less than a minute."

"What were you going to ask?"

"After, I'll ask it after. You know what to do now, right?"

The clock at the gate to Elder Park started to chime. The lights of Adelaide continued to shine in the night around us in the distance.

I glanced up at the moon one last time. If I remembered anything, it would probably be the rabbit I swear hopped in front of the moon. After a shake of my head, I squeezed Kane's hand.

"For me, the answer is my name: Mei," I said.

"And my answer is Kane, because that's my name, so don't wear it out."

"Oh, my goodness, I haven't heard that since primary school," I said.

Our laughter that followed filled the air as the ninth lantern floated towards the portal and joined the others. Together, the lanterns rotated around the golden doorway. On the other side of it, I could see the landscape blur as a portal swirled and ebbed before it settled. I People sat on the ground with their heads raised to the sky. Their faces lit with each explosion of colour that illuminated the sky.

I turned to Kane and held out my hand. He stepped close and his fingers curled around mine. For a moment, we just looked at each other and smiled.

"Ready to go home?" he asked me.

"Definitely," I replied.

We walked up the steps into the rotunda. The lanterns continued to spin. All we had to do was step through the portal and we were home. A relief it was so close and yet I had enjoyed the time with Kane. Everyone looked so happy watching the fireworks.

I felt Kane's fingers tighten around mine.

"You okay?" he asked.

I nodded and breathed in the air. "Let's do this."

We stepped through the portal, and our shadows faded from the grass before us. Above us the fireworks lit the sky, and I raised my gaze to watch as they changed the darkness into a rainbow. I squeezed Kane's hand and leaned my head against his shoulder.

"We're back. We are really back," I whispered.

The scent of the fireworks and the chatter of people, everything that was so completely normal. It seemed as if no time had passed since we had drunk the elixir.

"Was any of it real?" I asked.

"It has to have been, otherwise I wouldn't know what you were talking about and we probably wouldn't be standing here holding hands."

"Very good point."

"You know, I never believed in magic. Not really, but after tonight I think I could believe in anything at all."

I moved my gaze to Kane to find him looking down at me. His hair moved in the night breeze as the brown glowed red, blue, and yellow in time with the fireworks.

"Do you think it was really the elixir? That somehow Ying Yue planned it all?"

Kane ran his free hand through his hair and I suppressed a laugh at the nervous gesture.

"I think it's better not to question what an old lady who can turn herself into a rabbit does." He smiled at me.

"I have to agree on that point."

"Can I get you to agree with another?" Kane's words staggered out of his mouth.

"Depends what it is?"

"That if we kissed, it would be a good idea."

A couple of hours ago, I would have blushed and probably looked for somewhere to hide. Not that I wouldn't have wanted it, but because of how long I had wanted it. Now though, after solving all those riddles together, working together, talking together; now I had no fear of feeling embarrassed or silly.

"I would agree with that."

"Really?" His eyebrows rose. "Sorry, I mean, I hoped you would agree, but... well, anything could happen."

His hand reached down and came to a rest on my shoulder. I pushed myself up onto my tippy-toes as his face moved closer to mine. Kane's warm breath caressed my cheek. The familiar sandalwood scent assured me I was safe.

I breathed out before I closed my eyes just before his lips brushed mine. Soft and warm. I returned the kiss when it came. The fireworks I heard in my ears were probably above in the sky, at least I thought they were, but I couldn't be positive. Even when we moved apart, I saw Kane's wide grin; my own expression probably looked a little goofy with the range of emotions flooding through my mind and feelings through my body.

"Hey, are you two lovebirds ever going to come and sit down? I mean, hello, you've missed nearly all the fireworks!" Lucy called out.

"Busted," Kane said.

I turned to see Lucy standing with her hands on her hips. Kane's hand fell away from my shoulder, but his hand continued to hold mine as we walked over to the group.

"Next time you two want to just up and disappear like that, you tell someone, okay? There was like a whole ten minutes we couldn't see you and he was completely useless. Like who falls asleep as fireworks start?"

I moved my head to glance down to see Jace lying on the grass with his eyes closed; a mooncake still held firmly in his hand.

"Trust me, if there is something worth seeing, he'll probably miss it."

"I can't figure out what on earth could have happened in the ten minutes. I mean, we all knew you liked each other, but how come ya'll look like you've been dating for weeks?"

I opened my mouth to answer, but I had no idea how to explain the night without them thinking I was crazy. When I looked at Kane, I saw him shrug his shoulders and shake his head.

"I don't know, Lucy. Maybe it was something we drank."

"Ugh, that elixir was so good. Mei totally remind me to ask Miki how she made that on Monday at school."

Overhead, the last of the fireworks faded away and, after a short applause, the surrounding people began the exodus of the park. Extra buses were on tonight, but I wasn't in a hurry to get on the first one.

Kane nudged Jace's back with his shoe, and I looked up at the sky. The moon shone down from above. I would have to ask Lao Lao about Chang'e, as I had a feeling there was more to that story than what I'd been told.

All the people seemed happy with the night, including my granddaughter, who sold all the elixirs we had made. Her parents, of course, wanted the money to go into her savings account, but the girl earned it and should spend it on what she wanted. I smiled as she folded the cloth from the table and packed it away in the rolling case.

"I think that's the last of it, Nai Nai," she said.

Miki spoke so well in Mandarin; it pleased me greatly. I closed my eyes and gave a slow nod. My eyelids were so heavy. When my son arrived with the car, all I wanted was a nice nap in the backseat as we went home.

"A good night. A very successful night this year," I said.

"Because we sold it all?"

My lips curled into a smile. "Because the tale ended in happiness rather than parting. Anytime that happens is a good job." I paused to wiggle my toes under the woollen blanket.

"What tale Nai Nai?" Miki asked.

I looked once more as people passed by the empty table. A little giggle escaped my lips as two teens held hands as they passed by. Both smiled my way, but didn't stop. Nothing warmed my heart faster than that of love and a shared secret.

"Nai—"

Her attention diverted to her phone as a message came in. *Probably my son who can't find anywhere to park*. Such technology could never rival that of real magic. The magic of the moon flowed through my veins and maybe one day my granddaughter would understand. Tonight though, Chang'e would smile down on me from the moon, knowing I did a good job.

Thank you *for taking a chance on me!*

I value all my readers immensely.

If you have a moment,

please leave a rating or review

on your favourite platform.

Find information on all my books on my website

JenniWardAuthor.com

YA Books

Good Luck, Bad Luck

The Burden

YA Novelettes

Good and Evil Magic

Something Right

Spells After Dark (Blackbriar Academy)

Then, They Were Crows (coming 2023)

Please enjoy the following chapter from my

novel ***Good and Evil Magic.***

BONUS

JENNI WARD

GOOD AND EVIL
MAGIC

SHE CAN ONLY HAVE ONE

Good and Evil Magic : Chapter 1

My finger tingled with each tick. The clock's hand refused to move at a speed I could be content with. I mean, it *seemed* to be the speed of a sloth on a bad day. I diverted my gaze and hoped it would move faster because it clearly intended to punish me for watching. I only had to point my finger and send a little bit of magic towards time to end the torture. Seriously, the teacher droned on and on and if I had to listen too much more, I would be tempted to rip the door from the frame and fly out of there.

Beside me, Mina tapped her pencil on the desk. Okay, so it wasn't exactly on the desk, instead she inflicted the beating on her notepad that lay on the desk. It made enough noise to compete with the clock in irritating my nerves. If anyone else did it, I would seek revenge. Mina was my best friend and we would never fall out over something so trivial, right?

A deep breath didn't calm my desire to escape. My gaze fell to the clock again. If I tried something, there was no guarantee that it would actually do what I wanted it to. That's the thing. Witches aren't proficient at casting spells and curses the day they're born. Even with hard work, my skills still leaned on the dodgy side.

Sometimes I imagined what it would have been like if my parents had actually taken the time to teach me the spell casting stuff. I hadn't minded my parents allowed me to learn by trial and error as a kid. They'd always been careful to clean up any mess I made that I couldn't myself, and I need to be honest though, they rarely needed to. The older I'd gotten, the more I wanted to have a bit more guidance, so I didn't look like such an idiot when everything went wrong.

The thought lingered even as I glanced at Mina seated beside me. Mina had been on the receiving end of a spell gone wrong the previous year. Until then, I had been super careful to avoid friends being in the crosshairs. My goal had been to help her, seriously. When I had seen her wearing the crown, I just wanted to make it sparkle — just a little. Instead, her long hair looked like someone dumped a tonne of glitter into it, which is the reasoning I used when I pretended to throw glitter at others.

I had spread the disaster of my magic around. One time, Dylan had decided to be more of an annoyance than usual. A little cramp in his leg had been the intention. Instead, he limped around for days and had been benched during the football final. Of course, he told everyone that the doctor had diagnosed some rare type of growth at the bottom of his foot. That had made me smile because a horse's hoof certainly fell into the rare category, but he should be grateful he'd only been acting like a donkey's arse rather than a pile of shit. See, things could always be worse.

After so long at school, the end of the year seemed like the best Christmas present I could get. Just a few months until I would start my final year as a senior; after that, I could get out of this country town and conquer the world!

Before all that would be something else: Halloween. I know Halloween comes every year and people think it's just the same thing with different costumes. For humans, that all may be true, but for me this year I turned seventeen. Every witch gets to find out exactly the type they will be on their seventeenth Halloween. My parents hadn't expanded on what it all entailed, but I'd waited for this moment my whole life and I hoped it wouldn't disappoint.

Halloween was only a few days away and so far, I hadn't seen my parents make any preparations, but I suspected they were busy doing something. Things like conversations that ended when I walked into the room, strange lumps under blankets with my parents standing in front, smiling like they'd tried something illegal. Still, with my parents behaving like kids, it could be just a tad cute.

"Man, does he never shut up?" Mina said as she sat beside me.

"I'm sure he does when he has food in his mouth," I replied.

"Are you sure about that? I think I want to see proof. I mean, he just goes on and on like some terrible date you can't abandon with a fake trip to the loo."

Silence. I looked up to see the teacher. He stared at us long enough to make me fidget. My gaze fell to my book to appear as if I had paid attention to the lesson. As I stared at the page, the letters and numbers grew legs and ran around in circles — cheeky buggers. If just one person could explain why on this green earth, we needed to know algebra other than it had become a legal form of torture; I dared that person to come forward.

He didn't speak for a few moments. Even with my attention on the page, I felt his gaze as it burned into the top of my head. Amusement sabotaged my nerves. My lip twitched on one side and I struggled to stop its mate from joining in.

I sighed as his monotone voice droned once again. He felt anyone could complete the basic algebra; he reckoned it couldn't be clearer. No way I'd ever agree with that, but I only had to survive the lesson.

The bell rang, and I closed my eyes. Freedom came at last. Mina moved fast to collect her stuff and get out the door. It took me longer to locate my pen wedged under the textbook.

"And with that sweet sound, we are free for the day," Mina said.

We were jostled around as students exited their classrooms. When we made it to our lockers, I pressed my thumb on the lock and opened the door; at least I didn't melt the lock anymore with magic. With the books relegated to the shelf, I grabbed my backpack and banished the books (and the homework too) to the solitude of darkness.

"I can't believe how long that history lesson went," Natalie declared. She rested against the locker beside mine.

"Yeah, well, try ending with maths. It's not exactly a riveting celebration for the end of the day." I sighed as I shut the locker door and checked my pockets for the lock. It couldn't have gone far.

"Oh, maybe I didn't have it so bad after all," Natalie said. Her books were still in her arms as she hugged them close to her body.

"Yeah, well ladies, I had English lit last, so all your sympathy should be reserved for me."

My head tilted back at the sound of his voice. *Why did Mason have to get a locker near mine? There had to be at least thirty others nearby he could have had, but no, he got the one right next to mine.* Natalie moved to my other side to allow him access to his unlocked cave of despair.

"In case you hadn't noticed, this is a private conversation," I said.

Mason leaned closer and his black hair swayed forward. "Then you all need to talk in quieter voices."

"Just... Wait, is that my lock?"

The corner of Mason's mouth twitched. He raised his hand. The lock dangled from his middle finger. "What, this thing? Fairly certain this one is mine."

I reached out, but he moved quicker. My feet scuffed the lino floor as my hand found my locker and saved me from hitting the ground. Still, Mason hooked the lock onto his locker and clicked it shut; his gaze never left me.

"I have a key, you know," I said.

His head moved closer, and I felt his breath on my ear as he said, "Not to that one you don't. Maybe check your pocket."

I watched Mason as he walked down the corridor. When he turned a corner, I straightened myself up. I reached into my jacket pocket and located my open lock. That made little sense; I *never* put my lock in there. My gaze trailed back to the corner. My finger tingled, and I curled them into a ball before I exacted the revenge that niggled in my mind.

"Anyway, I have some good news, ladies," Natalie said behind me.

My fingers relaxed. I slipped the lock in place and waited for the subtle click. Still, despite that sound, I gave it a firm yank — it held fast. I glanced towards Natalie and Mina, who were looking at the notebook in Natalie's hand. I shuffled to the side to block any potential view in case what I was about to do went wrong. With my fingers wrapped around the lock, I closed my eyes. *Make this lock stay nice and tight and if someone dares give them a fright.* My fingers released the metal. I turned to face my friends with my eyes open and a smile on my face - just like any good witch would.

"Come on then Natalie, let's hear it." I leant against the locker and could feel the lock dig into my back.

"Sure you're finished swooning?" Mina nudged me in the side.

"Hilarious." I bit my tongue and glowered at her, but I only got a giggle in return.

"Okay, best you say something before two friends decide to have a fight to the death." Mina finally broke eye contact and opened her locker to discard what was in her arms. She closed the door and turned to face Natalie.

How does she survive without a lock on the damn thing? I had tried the whole trusting people not to pinch stuff my first year at high school. I learnt fast that a lock saved you many times from being interrogated by a teacher about why you didn't have certain items in your possession; items that would then frequently reappear in my locker after the lesson. I had strong suspicions but no proof... yet.

"Well, I just got invited to a group that is meeting up for the Halloween walk. You know, a bit of trick of treating, a little of socialising. Okay, it's basically just to get away from the parents, but you know, it should be fun and you're invited too," Natalie said.

Before I considered the idea, Mina replied, "Anything to avoid having to see what my brother gets up to. Oh my, like you would swear that once you hit twenty, you would be so over Halloween, like he is supposed to be a grownup—sort of—but he dresses up and suddenly it's like he's a freaking five-year-old high on sugar."

"The joy of having siblings, which is one of those things I am happy to be without. Definitely not missing out on a thing," I replied. My smile widened, and she countered with a death stare.

"So, you girls are in then?" Natalie asked.

"Like you even need to ask." Mina pushed herself off the locker and stood beside Natalie.

"Awesome. So, we're all going to meet tomorrow night at about five. You know, near that old cemetery gate? The one with that piece of the metal missing? That's where they've decided it would be the perfect place for us to start."

"How predictable and cliché." I joined them and we walked down the corridor. "I guess we're expected to get all dressed up as well, yes?"

"Of course, what would Halloween be if went just the way we look every other day? Halloween is all about being someone or something different. To get a feel for what it would be like to be evil or good, there's a few I can think of that are not acquainted with knowing what that is," Natalie said.

"Yeah, and I know who would be first on that list for Vania."

I looked over at Mina, but she continued to stare ahead. The corner of her mouth lifted though as Natalie nudged her. We walked out of the door and into the cool air. It smelt like rain; goose bumps appeared on my skin and I tugged down on my sleeves.

We parted away at the gate with hugs and waves. The walk home would give me a chance to think about how I could manage the night. I would be in my witch ceremony outfit anyway for later on, so all I had to do was dress up in that early. Anyway, what better outfit to wear on Halloween than a witch?

Continue Vania's Halloween night in *Good and Evil Magic*.
Available now in ebook and paperback.

Here's your chance to read more romance around the August Moon / Mid-Autumn Festival / Mooncake Festival theme! Check out all these fantastic stories by your favourite Contemporary, Fantasy, Paranormal, and Sci-fi authors.

Unlock the Angel by Calla Zae

Cathy just wants to focus on her career and the August Moon Festival, but one kiss from an angel changes everything for her. Can he keep her safe while the evil swarms them?

Over the Moon(cake) for You by Isla Chiu

When my family finds out that a corporate chain bakery is going to open right next to our shop, we can't help freaking out. I try to stay positive and tell my family that there's no way a soulless corporate chain's mooncakes

could compare to Grandma's.

But even without competition, our little bakery is

struggling to make ends meet.

When a gorgeous guy asks me out on a date, I think there might be some August Moon magic in the air.

Then I discover that he's the owner of the corporate chain bakery next door...

The Moon is a Tennis Ball by Ticana Zhu

Jake and Lana are childhood friends. As they enter high school, their lives change. They struggle to reconcile growing apart. The Asian Mid-Autumn fest in their town celebrates the "August Moon"--the revered harvest moon in Asian culture. Events leading to this holiday give both a chance at seeing themselves and their desires clearer.